The Artist and the Architect

Demi

Henry Holt and Company

New York

For the appreciation of others' talents

Library of Congress Cataloging-in-Publication Data
Demi
The artist and the architect / Demi.
Summary: In ancient China a jealous artist plots
to eliminate the favorite architect of the Emperor.
Trade ISBN: 0-8050-1580-9
Reinforced Library Binding ISBN: 0-8050-1685-6
[1. Artists—Fiction. 2. China—Fiction.] I. Title.
PZ7.D3925Ar 1991
[E]—dc20   90-40936

Printed in the United States of America
on acid-free paper. ∞

1 2 3 4 5 6 7 8 9 10

Once upon a time in China there was a wise and just Emperor who greatly appreciated the arts.

He built wonderful

halls and pavilions to house

the treasures of the land.

Two gifted men, one an artist,
the other an architect, served
him well.

But the artist grew jealous of the architect and began to pick quarrels with him.

As the days went by, the artist's jealousy became so great that he could not tolerate the architect any longer. And so the artist contrived a way to get rid of the architect.

He prepared a piece of sheepskin,

making it appear very old,

and painted strange decorations

with mystic writing all over it.

He presented it
to the Emperor, saying, "This
parchment fell down from Heaven!"

The Emperor examined it, but was unable to make anything out of the strange decorations and mystic writing. He asked the artist, "Can you read what it says?"

The artist studied it, and at length said, "This is a letter sent by your deceased father, the former Emperor. It says that he has been fortunate and is quite happy in Heaven. He asks that you send him a good architect immediately to build a palace for him, as nobody there knows how.

"The method for sending the architect is clearly stated. A large pile of wood and a match are all that are required. The architect will rise with the smoke. After the Heavenly palace is completed, he will be sent down to earth again."

The architect was summoned and told about the message from the former Emperor. "This is the trickery of the artist!" he thought.

Yet he said, "Very well. I ask only that your Highness grant me a week to settle my household affairs."

The architect returned to his family and had his servants dig a tunnel from his house to the northeast corner of the open square where all the public functions took place.

Then he ordered them to
loosen one of the large stone
slabs there.

After a week had passed, the architect appeared before the Emperor. Instructions were given for firewood to be placed on the northeast corner of the square. The architect sat on a stone slab while the wood was piled around him.

The Emperor and his officials watched while the match was applied. Smoke began to roll out, and rapidly enveloped the architect. At that moment he fell forward, pretending to be dead.

Unseen by the crowd, the architect rapidly lifted the stone slab and crept into the tunnel,

escaping to a secret room

in his house.

The spectators admired his fortitude. They believed he had ascended to Heaven,

since there was no trace of his charred remains. His relatives wept openly, to demonstrate their grief.

The architect stayed in the secret room for a month. Taking only light food and a little tea, he became quite thin, and the dark, sunless room gave his skin a deathlike pallor.

In this secret room he had hidden a robe of white silk, a box of costume jewelry, and a few lengths of translucent gauze, which he now made into a turban. Putting on this odd costume, he looked like an apparition, and in it he went to see the Emperor.

"You have returned!" the Emperor exclaimed. "How is my father? Did you finish the palace? Are there any instructions from him?"
The architect nodded, and silently presented a letter that read:

My dear son,
Thank you for your architect's help. The palace is now completed, but the walls, ceiling, and beams need decorations. There is no gifted artist here, so I am asking you to send someone. Use the same method as before.

The artist was thereupon

summoned.

He was greatly surprised
to see the pale, unearthly looking
architect, and concluded that
he really had gone to Heaven
and returned.

And with this comforting
thought, he said in a grandiose
manner, "I'm willing to go! Let
me rise with the smoke!"

The fire had already been lit—
but this time there was no
loosened stone.

Did the architect have a change
of heart, and forgive the artist
for his treachery?
An old proverb says, "The small
man harbors an envious spirit;
the great man rejoices in the
talents of others."